YSOBELLA BLACK

SHADOWY

A STRYGOI WITCHES & VAMPIRES COMPANION SHORT STORY
VIKTORIA'S PREQUEL

Table of Contents

WORKS BY THE AUTHOR

All of my stories and series, except for Alix in Wonderland and Raven Chronicles, are a different aspect of my Dragaverse, but can be read and enjoyed as standalone.

Stories by Ysobel Black
(Nice/Sweet Versions)

Bakery Street Cozy Mysteries

Paranormal Cozy Mysteries
The Lyrical Lycanthrope

Fairy Tales With a Twist

Retellings of fairy tales, myths, and stories you only thought you knew.
The Crimson Hood & the Alpha of Wolves
The Ice Maiden & the Princes of Diamonds

Holiday Hullabaloo

Love in Ashana can be tricky, but twelve days of chaos result in paranormal happily-ever-afters.
A Penghou in a Pine Tree
Two Tatzelwurms
Three French Bêtes
Four Ceffyl Dŵr
Five Golden Wings

Six Grootslangs Playing
Seven Spawns a-Swimming
Eight Maenads Mixing
Nine Lazy Dragons
Ten Swords a-Sneaking
Eleven Pixie Potions
Twelve Lovers Loving

Pohjola Maidens

The Maidens of Pohjola are free, heading for the human world, and looking for love.
Dream's Sleeper: Lemminki

Strygoi Witches & Vampires

Join an Ildum of vampires over 10,000 years of history and mythology as they find their Dragăs — witches who make their hearts beat and restore their souls.
Ember's Light: Stryx
Viktoria's Shadow: Jael
Myth's Legend: Norrix
Bijou's Cure: Zeke
Musette's Fate: Idris

Strygoi Witches & Vampires Companion Stories

Shadowy — Viktoria's prequel (companion novella)
Echo's Answer: Lachlan (companion novel)

COLLECTIONS/BOX SETS

Holiday Hullabaloo
DAYS 1-12

Strygoi Witches & Vampires
COLLECTION ONE, BOOKS 1-4

Stories by Ysobella Black
(Naughty/Steamy Versions)

Alix in Wonderland

A reverse harem (MFMMM) retelling of Alice in Wonderland.
Madness of the Hatter

Bakery Street Mysteries

Paranormal Cozy-ish Mysteries
The Lyrical Lycanthrope

Fairy Tales With a Kink

Retellings of fairy tales, myths, and stories you only thought you knew.
The Crimson Hood & the Alpha of Wolves
The Ice Maiden & the Princes of Diamonds

Grove of Bandrui

Immortal Druids search for their Maités.
Druid of Oaks
Druid of Apples

Harom & Aneja

Witches choose three men to form their Haroms as they become Aneja
— Walkers in magic. Reverse Harem (MFMM)
RealmWalker
BeastWalker

Magical Love in London

Regency London with a Paranormal twist
A Marriage of Inconvenience

Oubliette

Paranormal Short and Steamy Stories
Selkie
Merrow

Pohjola Passions

The Maidens of Pohjola are free, heading for the human world, and
looking for love.
Dream's Sleeper: Lemminki

Raven Chronicles: Phoenix Rising

An epic spanning generations — the battle for the Raven Throne is full
of sex, intrigue, and betrayal.
First Generation

Souls Lost & Found

Under a Blue Moon, star-crossed lovers get a second chance for their love to shine.
The Egyptian

Utopia Pack Shifters

A pack of shifters find their Fateds.
Unyielding

Vampires & Strygoi Witches

Join an Ildum of vampires over 10,000 years of history and mythology as they find their Dragăs — witches who make their hearts beat and restore their souls.
Ember's Light: Stryx
Viktoria's Shadow: Jael
Myth's Legend: Norrix
Bijou's Cure: Zeke
Musette's Fate: Idris

Vampires & Strygoi Witches Companion Stories

Shadowy — Viktoria's Prequel (Companion Novella)
Echo's Answer: Lachlan (Companion Novel)

Xuterias: Xov & Xau

Enemies to Lovers Paranormal Romances
Poisoned Heart

Yuletide Chaos

Short Paranormal Romances about finding love in mystical Ashana.
A Penghou in a Pine Tree
Two Tatzelwurms
Three French Bêtes
Four Ceffyl Dŵr
Five Golden Wings
Six Grootslangs Playing
Seven Spawns a-Swimming
Eight Maenads Mixing
Nine Lazy Dragons
Ten Swords a-Sneaking
Eleven Pixie Potions
Twelve Lovers Loving
12 Days of Chaos Box Set

COLLECTIONS/BOX SETS

Three First in a Series

FATED – Three Firsts
Ember's Light:Stryx
RealmWalker
Poisoned Heart

Five First in a Series

<u>FATED – Five Firsts</u>
Ember's Light:Stryx
The Crimson Hood & the Alpha of Wolves
RealmWalker
Dream's Sleeper: Lemminki
Poisoned Heart

<u>Vampires & Strygoi Witches</u>
<u>COLLECTION ONE: BOOKS 1-4</u>

<u>Yuletide Yearnings</u>
DAYS 1-12

<u>https://ysobellablack.com/newsletter</u>[1]

---

1. https://ysobellablack.com/newsletter/

1,001 YEARS AGO

CHAPTER ONE

SHADOW

AT THE TOUCH OF FINGERTIPS stroking her hip, Shadow turned from her side to her back and sighed with a smile. In the Soul Path's shimmering green light streaming through her bedroom window, her shadow lover took form and braced his naked body over hers as he always did when he came to her. And, as always, his face remained hidden in a dark shadow even she couldn't penetrate. She caressed his strong jaw, muscled shoulders and thighs. Every ridge on his abdomen.

He kissed and touched her with lips and fingers that knew exactly how soft a caress or urgent a demand to use in order to spike her need for him.

Shadow loved his kisses. Slow. Leisurely. Exploring with his tongue. Tasting with his lips. Sucking on her lower lip and grazing it with the sharp points of his teeth. Taking her mouth in another deep, soul-penetrating kiss.

Even though he always gave her pleasure no matter what they did together, his kisses felt more real than anything else.

Spreading her knees in invitation, Shadow wrapped her thighs around his waist. As he settled between her legs, she felt the head of his cock at her entrance, then he pressed into her. She ran her nails down his back and kissed him harder.

He thrust with deep strokes. Her body hummed with pleasure as he rolled his hips and increased his speed.

She tossed her head back and his teeth grazed her neck as he slammed into her.

He pulled back, shoved her knees to her chest and held them there while he bucked into her harder, abs and chest and arms flexing with every movement, until an orgasm ripped through her.

She never wanted it to end.

But as he always did, her shadow lover disappeared.

SHADOW NUDGED DREAM with an elbow, trying to divert her attention from the antics of their other eleven sisters in their shared dressing room. The crystalline clear walls reflected blue-eyed, platinum blondes holding up white gowns to themselves from every possible angle. "Let's get out of here."

She felt restless after her latest encounter with her shadow lover. He'd left her with a longing for something more that she had in life.

Dream's eyes widened in astonishment as she turned her attention from the parade of their sisters to Shadow. "But... we can't leave now! We're choosing our dresses for the day, and how to do our hair. It's the most important thing we have to do!"

The same as they did every day. After hours of debate, all thirteen of them would keep their hair loose, tumbling in straight lines over their shoulders to their waists. And as they did every day, all of them would exchange floor-length, frilly nightgowns for a sleeveless, flowy, white dress and matching slippers.

Almost everything was white in their mother's realm of Pohjola. The ever present snow. The walls and the floors of the ice palace they lived in.

The clothes all Louhi's daughters dressed in. The slippers they wore on their feet.

The only exceptions were the blue sky, the black sea, some of the black or gray soul birds, and the green, grassy meadow and forest areas the birds lived in.

"We're all going to wear these white dresses and our hair down." Shadow waved an arm at her sisters. "The same as we do every day."

"Don't be silly. We don't choose the same thing *every* day."

Shadow sighed. Yes, they did. Well, unless a kidnapping interrupted their routine. As Maidens of Pohjola, men sought them as trophies and status symbols.

Already dressed, Shadow shoved a gown and a pair of slippers at Dream. "It's my turn to be kidnapped. If you come with me, you can take my place."

"Really?" Dream squealed and clapped a hand to her mouth. She snatched the clothes and stood. "Okay. Let's go."

Their soft, white slippers made no noise as they walked along the winding corridors through the palace to the wooden drawbridge. The guards, dressed in white armor and capes, observed them go, but didn't stop them.

Shadow hooked her elbow with Dream's and guided her sister toward the forest of tall evergreen trees wearing a dusting of snow. Dream often lost track of where she was and wandered off. As they crossed the meadow, the Sielulintu, enormous swans large enough to carry people on their backs, honked and lowered their heads for attention.

After spending some time scratching itchy beaks and smooth ruffled feathers, Shadow led Dream through the forest. It was hard to predict where a kidnapper would show up, but the forest usually provided excellent opportunities. Plenty of trees for an abductor to hide behind, and the trail was wide enough for a horse.

Snowy owls hooted from the trees. Arctic foxes watched them with curious eyes. A mother polar bear with two small cubs trundled across their path. The small bears rose on their hind legs and rumbled ferociously.

The bears were adorable rather than frightening, since the Goddess of Witchcraft and Death would never allow harm to come to her daughters.

The rhythmic pounding of hooves on hard packed earth made Shadow jerk her head up. The owls went silent as snow. The foxes disappeared into their holes. The mama bear herded her babies to safety. "Dream, a kidnapper is here." *Finally.* "Get ready."

Dream blinked, snapping out of a trance. Releasing her, Shadow stepped to the side of the trail.

The hoof beats faded. Where was the stupid man going?

Whatever diversion he galloped off to caused too long of a delay. Dream's eyes went distant, and she stood in the center of the path, head tilted to the side.

A gray cloud manifested behind Dream, and a brown war horse galloped out, carrying his armored rider. The steed didn't show any signs of slowing as he barreled down the trail. When Dream didn't move, the horse reared, front legs thrashing in the air.

"Dream!" Shadow rushed from the trees and pushed her sister out of the way of the flashing hooves. She held onto Dream's arms, trying to keep her upright.

Hooves slammed to the ground beside them. An armored arm snaked around Shadow's waist, bodily ripping her away from her sister, who fell backward. "Dream! Wake up!"

The man deposited Shadow in front of him on the horse and locked her in place with one arm. She twisted in his grasp to see Dream picking herself up off the ground.

While her sisters enjoyed being stolen away, every time a kidnapper took Shadow, a sense of dread set her heart beating too fast and her breath catching in her lungs as they squeezed in fear. *He can't hurt you. He can't hurt you.* The chant reassured her only a bit.

She tried indignation instead. "Stop the horse at once, you raakalainen. It's not my turn!"

The kidnapper ignored her. A fog bank opened to their left, and the man guided the horse toward it.

"Please, release me! Dream wants to go with you. You can still have your precious prize," Shadow grumbled. "We're all the same to you, anyway."

This was met with silence.

"Are you even going to tell me your name? Tell me how lucky I am to be your trophy? Brag about all your heroic deeds?"

More silence.

"You know, there is a point where the silent part of strong, *silent* type crosses a line."

They plunged into the fog.

Shadow sighed. Being kidnapped wasn't all it was cracked up to be anymore.

THEY EMERGED FROM THE fog at the foot of a castle. The horse galloped parallel to the gray brick wall while Shadow tried to adjust to the riot of sensations assaulting her. She squeezed her eyes shut against the bright colors, put her hands over her ears to block the sounds of screaming seagulls, waves crashing on rocks, and wrinkled her nose at the combination of smells — sweat from the man behind her and the horse beneath her, salt from the ocean, smoke and roasting meat from somewhere in the castle.

Before she could orient herself, the horse stopped, and her kidnapper dismounted, dragging her with him. He threw her over his shoulder. Shadow hated being carried this way. It was so undignified. And his armor dug into her stomach. He ran up a winding staircase in huge bounds, jarring her painfully each time he landed.

A wooden door creaked open, and she staggered as her world spun when he set her on her feet, turned and left. The door slammed behind him.

Shadow opened her eyes, stumbling toward a blur that could be a chair. She sat, rubbing her sore stomach as she blinked, her vision coming into focus.

He'd abandoned her in a round chamber, containing a four-poster bed stripped of bedding, a wardrobe, its open doors revealing a distinct lack of clothing, and a long table with two chairs, one on either end. A twin to the armchair she perched on sat across from a fireplace containing logs ready to be lit.

Overstuffed pillows and colorful carpets lay scattered on the floor.

No books. No games. Not even dreaded embroidery or some other frivolous activity these men thought abducted women should occupy themselves with. He'd taken her away from the boredom of Pohjola, only to leave her trapped here — bored.

A salt-tinged breeze blew long curtains into the room. Shadow stood and went to a window, pushing the light fabric aside to see where she was. Deep blue ocean stretched to the horizon. Windows on the other three walls gave her the same distant view. An island? If that was the case, escape from here wouldn't be easy.

Maybe that was the idea. He'd leave her here with nothing to do while he was off on some grand adventure and expect her to pine away, happy to see him when he returned and deigned to pay her attention.

Well, he was going to be in for a surprise!

Below her window, the gray wall enclosed several buildings other than the tower, their steep tiled roofs too far away for her to jump to. No escape that way.

The door slammed open. Shadow clutched at her heart and whirled as an army of people trooped into the room. Musicians wearing blue pants and tunics with gold piping, and carrying string instruments set up in front of one window. None of them looked at her or asked what she might like to hear. They just started playing — one of them warbling about beauty.

Women wearing long gray dresses with matching kerchiefs on their heads carried in bedding and a variety of fancy, colorful gowns. So he intended for her to play dress up?

Boys and girls followed them, bringing in platters of food that they set on the long table, then scurried out the door without glancing in her direction.

No one looked at or talked to Shadow. Had he forbidden any contact? Shadow stepped toward the woman who seemed to be in charge — she spoke to the others in harsh whispers and managed the proceedings by jabbing the air with an imperious finger.

"Hello." Shadow smiled. There was no point in being angry with these women. They were only doing their jobs, and they hadn't kidnapped her. "Thank you for all…" — she waved an arm — "this. Can you tell me where I am?"

The women froze in place for a moment, then burst into a flurry of activity. The one in charge tsked and muttered, "No point in talking to this one either." In seconds, the maids filled the wardrobe, made the bed neatly, and fled, leaving Shadow with the musicians.

What did that mean? This one? No point? Did this kidnapper want to hurt her? The sense of dread she'd been suppressing threatened to overwhelm her. Did this one think her even less special than an interchangeable Maiden of Pohjola? Anyone would do, as long as someone was kept in this tower?

Shadow sighed. Well, at least the translation magic worked. What would it be like to be kidnapped and not be able to understand anyone? That thought sent a shudder through her.

Maybe she should end this farce. She could always reach her mother. In Pohjola, the soul birds loved her. But what would she be going home to? Even though being away from home meant fighting back fear, sometimes the freedom found outside her mother's realm was worth being a little scared. Whenever she left Pohjola, her mind engaged, like she'd escaped the influence of some kind of spell.

That was a distinct possibility. Their mother was Louhi, Goddess of Witchcraft and Death. It could even be something in the water. Shadow's grandmother brewed Beer of Oblivion — a few sips of that, and a human would forget they'd ever existed. Her mother could have come up with a less potent version. She preferred her daughters... docile.

The melodies serenading her with words of love and her beauty may as well be songs about the love *of* her beauty. Shadow huffed and slumped against an overstuffed pillow on the bed. Instead of flattering, the music drove her toward insanity. Using the magic she'd been named for, she formed the nearest shadow into a polar bear. It slid over the walls and floor, encroaching on the corner the noise emanated from. "Go away!"

The music stopped on a discordant jangle as the musicians, appropriately appreciative of their unappreciative audience, left without a backward glance. Shadow rose and paced, berating herself. She should have asked where she was before she sent them away.

There was an ongoing bet with her sisters on how far the next kidnapper would take them from Pohjola. Whoever was taken the farthest won the chance to plan their next escape attempt. But that's all they did. Plan. There was no point in leaving Pohjola. Their mother always retrieved them.

The quiet felt even more stifling after the first few moments, but a distant sound intruded into her gilded cage. Something metal crashed against other metal. A sword smashing against armor? Had her kidnapper returned?

Leaving her room, Shadow followed the clashing sounds down the stairs and through the castle. They led her outside to a courtyard not visible from her balcony or windows.

A tall man wearing a metal helmet, leather pants, knee-high boots, and a baggy tunic, sword in hand, attacked another man dressed in a full suit of armor.

Her kidnapper was bulkier than these men, so who were they? Soldiers in his army? Then why weren't they on the quest with him?

The man lunged, sword blurring in a series of blows that smacked against the armor. He danced from one position to the next with graceful footwork while the armored man staggered under the barrage.

Shadow longed for the ability to wield a sword like that. She'd never be kidnapped again. If she could teach her sisters to fight, too, maybe none of them would be taken, and they could live their own lives instead of being suffocated in the heavy-handed protection of their mother in Pohjola.

The man spun, and Shadow gasped. The helmet didn't have a full face plate — this man was a woman!

After a brief hesitation, the woman let her momentum break their locked gazes. She finished her turn and kept up her attack. Swinging low, she took her adversary's ankles from under him and sent him clanking to the ground.

The warrioress removed her helmet, shook out her long red hair and laughed. "I ken yer the third lass this week!"

Her armored opponent rolled side to side on the ground like a turtle unable to turn over. The woman reached down, hauled him to his feet, and sent him clattering away.

"What happened to the other two, um, lasses?" The question was out before Shadow realized she might not want to know.

The woman waved her sword in the air. "Sent them home, didnae I? He's been a bampot radge since he woke. Shipwrecked he was, and washed up on my island. Now he skedaddles aff fir bonnie lasses like he's awa' fir the messages."

Away for the messages? Shadow squinted at the woman while she waited for the words to make sense. Her mother's translation magic came back with nothing. "Why's he doing that? Kidnapping us?"

"I dinnae ken. Seems nice enough. He's some wizard son of Myrddin." She tapped her head with the tip of her sword. "I reckon his heid's mince, but he'll not harm ye."

"Oh." Leaving the strange behavior of the wizard man for the moment, Shadow asked, "Who are you? Where am I?"

"On the island of Hiort, west of Alba. I'm the Amazon."

"The Amazon?" That sounded more like a title than a name.

"Aye. 'Tis the only name ye'll get. Where's yer home?"

Alba had to be the farthest she'd ever been kidnapped! Maybe it would take her mother longer to find her at this greater distance. "I'm from Pohjola."

The Amazon shrugged. "I dinnae ken Pohjola."

"It's all right. My mother will find me and take me home. But before she does, will you teach me to fight?"

Face scrunched in a frown, the Amazon extended the tip of her sword to some flounces on the gown Shadow wore. "Feartie gowk."

"Um, what?"

"Ye dinnae look like a fighter."

"It's true I've never fought before, but I want to learn to fight like you." Shadow pointed to the sword. "With one of those. I'm sick of being kidnapped."

"Aye, I ken that. But ye'll not be fighting with this." She smirked and twirled her sword, offering it to Shadow.

The blade was heavy, and she couldn't hold the tip up, much less swing it with any accuracy. Shadow couldn't decide if the Amazon's expression was laughter or despair. Or maybe indigestion.

" 'Tis made only for me." The Amazon relieved Shadow of the sword and gave her a dagger.

Shadow made a few test stabs. "The smaller blade is better. I can use it. But it won't be much help against a man on horseback, or someone wearing armor. Is there something else I can try?"

The Amazon led the way through an arched wooden door with great black hinges and a stout bolt on the outside into an armory. Crossbows, flails, maces, bows, swords, daggers, and spears lined the walls.

She gaped. If she could learn to use all of these, or any of these, her life would be her own. But there wouldn't be time for that. Who knew when her mother would show up? "Which of these is the fastest to master?"

"Crossbow, maybe, if ye have the strength and aim. The rest won't happen quick." The Amazon shook her head, pity in her eyes. "Muscles and practice. 'Tis the way of things."

Shadow's heart sank. What good would any of this do her, anyway? Her mother would never allow her and her sisters to wander around Pohjola armed with weapons. She should have known better than to get her hopes up.

But the Amazon hadn't given up. "Do ye want the men tae die? Are ye willing tae kill them and maybe their horses tae be free? There's no point tae picking up any of these weapons if ye aren't prepared tae use them."

"I don't want to kill anyone, especially an animal forced to obey. I just want to protect my freedom to make my own choices."

The Amazon inclined her head. "Even the crossbow isn't for ye, then. Too easy to miss, tae easy tae hit a target ye dinnae intend."

"I don't know how much time I have left, and none of this will work!" Her mother kept her tame. Kidnappers treated her like an empty-headed souvenir. This woman, the only woman she'd ever seen able to fight, thought her weak.

Tears welled in Shadow's eyes, but she refused to let them fall. She whirled away from the pitying gaze of the Amazon, ending up facing her own shadow on the wall. It stood there, an ineffectual, flimsy, useless thing.

The Amazon's soft footsteps moved away.

Of course, she didn't want to see a stupid, silly girl cry. Shadow took a deep breath, a scream of frustration ready to rip from her throat. There had to be *something* she could do. Surely she wasn't meant to be a pathetic girl her whole life.

Her hands curled into fists, nails digging into the flesh of her palms.

Her shadow made fists, too.

The scream died in her throat. What if her shadows were only as strong as she was? All her life, she'd been content to let her mother do everything. Take care of her. Shadow had never tried to do anything for herself. *She* was weak — not her magic. She'd had the means to free herself her whole life, and never even tried!

Frustration fueled fury.

Shadow stalked out of the armory, caught up with the Amazon outside, and commanded her shadow to throw a punch, focusing the power and movements in her mind.

Her shadow lunged, arm outstretched, hand still in a fist. Powered by anger, Shadow turned her body and her shadow lifted off the wall, becoming something more solid than ethereal.

The blow that struck the Amazon's back was hardly more than a tap when it finally hit her, but the walls imprisoning Shadow's magic exploded. A dam burst inside her and power surged. She didn't have only her shadow, there were shadows *everywhere*.

The Amazon spun, looking surprised when Shadow wasn't immediately behind her. "What'd ye do? Toss a rock?" She shook her head. "Won't help, lass."

That one triumph wasn't enough. Shadow reached for the little bits of darkness around her. She had to do more to prove herself. Sweat broke out over her skin and a pain jabbed inside her skull. Her body trembled with effort as she tried to command shadows not her own. No, they were hers now. All shadows were. She felt it in her bones.

There was too much light this way. The other shadows felt... stuck. Her shadow stood ready. Not the useless, ineffectual, flimsy thing she thought it was — but the key to all the other shadows around her. Channeling magic through her shadow, she summoned it, holding back the whoop of joy when it stepped off the wall and merged with her. A new world overlaid itself on the world of light, and a cool, heady sensation of power filled her.

Most of the shadows were too far away to use as weapons themselves, but touched by her magic, she could give them form. Every shadow within her sight swayed unnaturally in the still air. Shadow tree branches elongated like claws.

The Amazon's shadow darkened and grew, looming over the woman it used to belong to, no longer mimicking her movements. The shadow of a rock near the Amazon's foot shifted to slide under her boot, making the woman stumble as she stepped back.

"What's wrong? Afraid of your own shadow?" Shadow called, her voice sounded new to her ears. No longer the light tone of a girl, but deeper — throaty and ethereal, like smoke.

Whirling with a triumphant yell, Shadow flung her arm at the startled Amazon. A whip of shadow darted across a wall, tore itself off and coiled around the other woman's wrist. It squeezed when Shadow closed her fist and retracted when she pulled her arm back, smashing the Amazon's wrist into the bricks.

Energy rushed out of Shadow as she strove to keep the other woman's wrist in place, pulling more shadows to build layers and strength.

Shouting a curse, the Amazon dropped her sword. She scowled, but her eyes gleamed. "Better. I ken we can work with that."

Elated, but exhausted, Shadow released her grip and collapsed to her hands and knees, her hold on the surrounding shadows slipping through her fingers. Her heart fluttered in her chest as panic threatened to overwhelm her. What if that was it and she couldn't do it again?

No. Inside her, her shadow dwelled in its new home. Calming her racing heart and breaths, Shadow lifted her head.

Metal scraped on rock as the Amazon bent to pick up her sword, watching her shadow the whole time. She backed away to stand before Shadow and offered a hand. "Lass, do ye need help up?"

Shadow accepted the stronger woman's help and was yanked to her feet. She swayed to get her balance. *One day, I'm going to be the stronger woman.*

COVERED IN BRUISES and sweat, wearing pants, boots, and tunic, hair braided tight rather than loose down her back, Shadow wielded her magic. The Amazon was a thorough teacher and a scrupulous observer. She'd figured out Shadow's strengths and weaknesses over the last three days, forcing her to think ahead and adapt to new circumstances.

Shadow crept forward, her back pressed to a wall in the courtyard, placing each booted foot with deliberate care to avoid making a sound. She eyed the dark silhouette of the tree branches. The Amazon was just around the corner. If Shadow called those shadows, the Amazon would see, follow them straight to Shadow and administer another thumping.

The Amazon didn't use her sword for the most painful lessons. Shadow hadn't known there were so many different ways for her body to hit hard surfaces.

Racking her brain, Shadow tried to think of something new. She studied the black silhouettes. To anyone else, they'd look one dimensional, but to her they held layers. Shadow cajoled a few of those to peel back exactly along themselves so it didn't look like they were moving. The black lightened to a dark gray, but otherwise, they appeared unchanged.

Coaxing the thin wisps down the back of the tree, Shadow pulled and shaped them on the ground, crafting a false shadow of the trunk. She wiped sweat from her brow. The painstaking work came to her easier, but it still required a lot of concentration.

Now her trap was set — time to be the bait. Shadow was still getting used to heavy boots on her feet. The Amazon made fun of the noise Shadow made in her boots often enough. She scuffed one sole on the ground and scampered to place the fake tree trunk between herself and the woman coming around the corner at a run. She ran silently, but Shadow had been stalked and caught by surprise often enough, her instincts were honed.

Shadow curved the shadows of the branches into talons, drawing the Amazon's attention to them.

"That's an old trick, lass." The Amazon gave the looming claws a wide berth as she approached. "I ken their reach. Ye'll have tae do better."

Backing up, Shadow determinedly kept her eyes off the fake shadow and drew the other woman after her. The Amazon preferred hand-to-hand combat. Three more steps... two... one. Shadow threw herself into a forward roll, remembering to tuck her shoulder this time so she didn't slam her face into the ground.

That had been embarrassing.

The Amazon laughed as she leapt into the air to jump over Shadow.

Shadow slapped a hand onto the fake trunk and channeled her magic into it. The shadow took form, becoming more solid but not too heavy. As soon as the Amazon landed, the trunk hit the backs of her knees, then lost its rigidity. Collapsing in a swirl of flexible fingers, the tendrils tangled around the woman's legs and brought her to the ground.

It didn't matter if Shadow was obvious now. Scrambling to her feet, she formed a curved sword from a different shadow. She gaped at the blade in her hand as an image of black eyes flashed in her mind, startling her so badly she almost lost her grip on her magic. Why had she picked that kind of weapon? Who had black eyes like that?

"A scimitar? Interesting choice."

Shadow narrowed her eyes. The Amazon sounded smug, and that usually resulted in bruises. "What do you know about scimitars?"

"I ken a guy." She smirked.

A vague memory scratched at Shadow's mind. Standing over her prone opponent, instinct brought her hands together. When she drew them apart, she held a curved blade in each hand. A sense of security and longing nearly sent her to her knees. Black eyes. Strong hands. A kiss? More than a kiss. Shadow caught her breath as heat and tingling swept through her.

What was happening? She blinked, trying to regain focus.

Fortunately, the blades also distracted the Amazon. Her brow creased as she stared at the weapons aimed at her.

Crossing the shadow blades over the Amazon's throat before she could recover, Shadow called, "Yield!"

The Amazon laughed. "Well done, lass. Well done."

Shadow grinned, reveling in victory — until the Amazon's arm moved in a blur and seized Shadow's ankle. The world upended, and she landed hard on her backside with a yelp.

"I didnae yield, lass. Physical fights arenae the only kind. Mind yer wits and words."

"Well done, Amazon. Well done."

"Now call off yer feartie gowk shadows."

SNOWFLAKES WHIRLED into the air. Shadow leapt from the armchair in her tower room and smoothed her hair as best she could. She hadn't felt her mother's magic coming this time and hadn't cleaned up after her last sparring session with the Amazon. The woman believed in ambushes and never-ending training.

Icy snow melted on the warm stone floor of her tower room, darkening spots on the multi-colored carpets. The flurry increased, and the Goddess of Witchcraft and Death stepped through her portal.

"You've been gone long enough, Shadow. It's —" Her mother narrowed her eyes and lifted a lock of Shadow's sweat-soaked hair. "Why are you disheveled? What are you wearing? Have you been harmed?" She shifted from her beautiful red-haired sorceress form to her gap-toothed hag form.

"No, mother. The kidnapper brought me here and left. These pants and tunic are all I could find to change into." That wasn't exactly a lie. Shadow had all the fancy gowns, and her stupid white dress, taken away and didn't know where they were.

Her mother glanced around the tower room, muttered something about kidnappers and pronouns, then relaxed, features returning to those of a beautiful woman. "Good. It's time to come home. Are you ready?"

"Oh, I'm ready, Mother." Ready to make this the last time she was ever taken somewhere not her choice.

CHAPTER TWO

LOUHI

FROM THE ICE THRONE atop the dais in her elaborately ice-carved crystalline throne room, Louhi eyed the leather-clad, muscle-bound, red-haired man on his knees in front of her. *What inane task can I assign him that won't end in him doing something stupid and getting himself killed?*

He was due to blubber pronouns at any moment, but hadn't worked up that much courage yet.

She pretended to ignore the bright flashes of color from the anteroom. A wisp of wind carried the words, muffled giggles, and girlish whispers of her daughters.

"Did you see the size of his pe—"

"Dream!" Rainbow shrieked, covering her mouth with her hand and glancing toward the throne room.

Louhi arched an eyebrow, but kept her eyes on the man in front of her. Maybe her girls were growing up after all. It had to happen at some point, despite her best efforts to insulate them from the world after what had happened to Shadow once.

Dream giggled again. "Pecs! He has so many muscles."

"What do you think Mother will make him do?"

"I don't know. I hope he doesn't die, though." Dream sighed. "He was nice."

The door closed without a sound as her daughters' boot steps receded.

Boots! Clomping all over the place.

Something was going on with all of her daughters. A quiet insurrection growing in the week since Shadow returned from that dreadful island full of sand, sun, noise, and garish hues.

The Maidens of Pohjola wore colors.

And pants.

And... ponytails.

Noisy steps of feet shod in boots rather than slippers clattered through the corridors at all hours. Unpleasant, blinding colors marred the icy landscape and startled the swans.

A guard, using far more pronouns than necessary, reported several swords missing from the armory. Really. Did every man think she was going to murder them? It was hardly her fault if heroes always took the smallest opportunity to get themselves killed.

And what were her daughters planning to do with the swords?

They gathered in small groups and plotted to escape more than usual. Her girls thought she didn't know, and she let them have their little game. When they got too far away from safety, Louhi retrieved them. They were in no way prepared to live outside Pohjola, and definitely not among... humans.

Louhi kept them sheltered, determined to protect them from the world, and themselves, until they proved capable. Instead of working toward independence though, her daughters seemed content to remain in Pohjola, their only excursions the kidnappings or half-hearted escape attempts.

The muscle-bound redhead in front of her stirred. Maybe things were about to become interesting. What was his name? Did it matter?

She liked to think her creativity boundless, but really, these heroic young fools seemed determined to die no matter how innocuous a quest she sent them on. As if a dead hero did her any good. She'd never get all her daughters out from underfoot if their prospects kept killing themselves.

This one was handsome enough, she supposed. One of her daughters would go in for the tall, long-haired, muscled type.

She shifted on her throne of ice. "Lemming —"

"I... You... My..."

And their endless *pronouns*. She resisted the urge to shift into her gryphon form and kill him on the spot.

Lemming cleared his throat — hopefully of pronouns. "My name is Lemminki."

She arched a brow at him.

He raised his head and met her eyes for a moment. "I mean no disrespect, Mistress of Pohjola, Goddess of Witchcraft and Death."

Two complete sentences. He knew his name and who she was. This one had some spine and more wits than most of them. Still, it wouldn't do to let him think she thought so. "Whoever." She waved a hand dismissively. "There is a black swan that swims the rivers of Tuonela. Your quest is to bring me a black feather."

That should be simple enough. Surely there was no need to die to pluck a feather from a swan. There were several of the birds right next to the palace, and they shed old feathers all of the time.

If Lemming wasn't so clever as to realize he could pick up one of those from the ground to fulfill his quest, getting into Tuonela would be tricky for him, but one didn't have to die to go to the underworld. She couldn't make it too easy to claim one of her daughters. There were enough besotted blackguards invading Pohjola when they thought she was an evil witch and would grind them up to use in one of her spells. If potential kidnappers thought she was getting soft, there was no telling how much chaos would descend on her orderly realm.

"Bring you a... feather?"

Perhaps her estimation of his wits had been premature and optimistic. Where were all the competent men, like that assassin with the two blades? Too bad he was human and long dead. What a sorry state of affairs — reduced to hoping a man could pick up a feather and not die.

Still, Lemming was pretty. Maybe Rainbow would be a suitable match for him. Or Dream. She had noticed the size of his... pecs.

"Did I stutter?" Louhi narrowed her eyes at him. "Well, off with you. Bodies don't keep forever, and I still have to finish disposing of the last hero who failed me."

Lemming's eyes grew round. He did a fair imitation of levitating from his knees to his feet and fled.

Chuckling, Louhi crossed to a window overlooking one of the few green expanses in her icy northern land of Pohjola.

The flock of Sielulintu, the black, white, and gray swans that carried souls, protecting them from being lost on the path of dreams during the journey to their afterlives, wandered the grassy meadow. They were tended to by ten... eleven... twelve...

Twelve daughters. One missing. These girls would be the death of her, always swanning off on the soul birds and getting in trouble.

"Mother!"

Ah, here was daughter thirteen. Louhi relaxed. "What is it, Memory?"

"There's a creepy old man watching us." A breeze blew Memory's long blonde hair back from her face. The slight wave to her tresses meant Memory's hair had been braided. So, she thought to play down her part in the rebellion, coming here wearing a white dress and her hair down. "He said he came here to find a wife. Shadow told him he had a delightful singing voice and now he's always spying on us!"

Not for the first time, Louhi wondered if she'd named her daughters like she'd named her sons there would be less of this nonsense. She never had these problems with Scab, Plague, Gout, Consumption, or Rickets.

"I'll take care of him."

"Thank you, Mother." Memory kissed her cheek and dashed out of the room to rejoin her sisters.

What shape should she use to deal with this latest interloper? The beautiful witch? No... he was here for a beautiful woman. She'd meet him as a gap-toothed hag. Maybe add a hump on her back and some warts this time.

That should be memorable enough.

But first, some intelligence was called for. She twirled her wrist in the air and held her palm flat. A small whirlwind floated over her hand. "What do you know of the old man watching the Maidens of Pohjola?"

A whispery voice spoke. "North wind heard his name is Väinämöinen, the first man, son of the sea. South wind heard he has a pleasant singing voice. East wind heard he is a Demi-God in search of a wife." The voice lowered. "West wind heard the last woman he wanted to marry drowned herself rather than be with him."

Perfect. Another charming prince of a man. "Bring him to me." She held her open palm out the window. The little whirlwind grew in size and spun away.

Louhi seated herself on her throne. The spinning winds rushed back in the window, dumping a man on the floor in front of her. He would not do for her daughters at all. He was old, had long white hair and a white beard that hung to his stomach. His eyes were calculating, and he carried himself with an air of entitlement and arrogance she didn't like. She waited until he straightened his clothing and stood.

"Well?" She made her voice thunder throughout the room. "What do you have to say for yourself?"

The man hunched his shoulders and looked at the floor. "I... You... He... They..."

So, the first man, son of the sea, was going to pretend to be a bumbling idiot. Louhi tapped her fingers on the arm of her throne. "Why is it, I wonder, that every man I catch skulking around my daughters thinks listing all of the pronouns he knows is some sort of answer, reason, or excuse? Because some tutor managed to beat basic language skills into you as a boy, you are entitled to what is mine?"

"I... You..."

Louhi sighed. "Yes, we've established those are two pronouns you are familiar with." She stood. "Let's cut to the chase, shall we? No quest for you. I'm of a mind to send you straight to Tuonela."

He dropped his idiot act. "No, wait! My name is Väinämöinen. My brother is a blacksmith — the greatest blacksmith! If you spare my life and allow me to wed one of your daughters, I will ask him to craft you a one of a kind treasure."

Only ask *his brother to craft one*, she mused. Not craft a treasure and give it to her. Well, two could play word games. "I see. So you think, rather than prove yourself worthy of one of my daughters, I should trade one to you in exchange for a trinket?"

"Not just any trinket. The Sampo!" He sang.

"On one side, the flour is grinding,
On another, salt is making,
On a third is money forging,
And the lid is many-colored.
Well, the Sampo grinds when finished,
To and fro, the lid is rocking.
Grinds one measure at the day-break,
Grinds a measure fit for eating,
Grinds a second for the market,
Grinds a third one for the store-house."

HE WOVE COMPULSION into his song. The nerve of this man! Louhi batted away the spell he tried to put her under using his voice.

A mill that churned out money, salt, and flour several times a day, though. She didn't have anything like that, or a need for money, but the cooks could use the salt and flour. And who knew? Maybe she could adjust it to make other things after she was rid of him.

"Very well. Contact your brother. He must forge the Sampo here in Pohjola. Our bargain will be you ask him to forge the Sampo. He will forge the Sampo and give it to me. It will be deemed my property. In return, I offer the choice of one of my daughters to you, and you will leave Pohjola alive. Agreed?"

"Agreed." Väinämöinen gave her a smarmy smile she didn't like. "I will send a message to my brother."

Taking a scroll and feather quill from his pockets, he scribed a note, muttering in irritation as the wind blew through the room, fluttering the paper. Finished, he crossed to the window and removed the kantele from his back. Strumming a few notes on the stringed instrument caused a seagull to appear, and he attached the note to its leg. "Take this to Ilmarinen in Kalevala, fast as the winds can carry you."

The bird flew south.

He faced Louhi. "I expect you will have appropriate accommodations and meals for me while we wait for my brother to arrive?"

"Of course." She inclined her head, twirled her wrist, and whispered instructions to the wind.

The doors blew open. Two large men dressed in suits of white armor complete with polar bear helms entered the room.

"Please escort our... guest to accommodation appropriate to his station."

"Excellent. I look forward to my stay here in Pohjola." Väinämöinen strutted out of the room.

"More fool you," Louhi muttered. Their instructions were to take him to the dungeon. His station where he was from didn't matter. Here in Pohjola, he was a stalker. She placed a blank scroll in front of the ashes of the fireplace. "What did his note say?"

Ash swirled over the paper, forming letters, then words.

Ilmarinen, worthy brother,
Thou the only skilful blacksmith,
Come see her wondrous beauty,
Her gold and silver garments,
See her robed in finest raiment,
Sitting on the rainbow,
Walking on clouds of purple.
Forge for Louhi, the magic Sampo,
Thou shalt win this bride of beauty;
And bring the lovely maiden
To thy home in Kalevala.

SO, VÄINÄMÖINEN THOUGHT to offer Rainbow to his brother. That hadn't been part of the deal. But she'd let it lie for now.

CHAPTER THREE

SHADOW

WHEN HER SHADOW LOVER came to her, he wielded twin scimitars. Was he the reason she'd thought about those swords when she fought with the Amazon? He'd never come to her with weapons before, but seeing the blades in his hands, she had no doubt they belonged there.

He spun the blades expertly as he stalked toward her. What was he going to do with those? Why had he brought them? He wouldn't hurt her, would he? Her lover was made of shadows, but she didn't control him. The appearances and departures were not her doing, nor were his actions when he was with her.

Her frilly nightgown tangled around her legs as she scrambled to slide off the bed. *Maybe I should start wearing pants to sleep.* She retreated as he strode forward, until her back hit the wall behind her. She pressed against it, summoning shadows to her fingertips.

The scimitars flashed. She closed her eyes and bit back a scream. Two gentle tugs at her shoulders and cool air flowed over her bare skin as her nightgown fell to the floor.

Then he was pressed against her. Her shadow lover's kiss was wild with urgent hunger. Rough, calloused hands cupped her face, then left a searing path down her body as he lifted her and carried her to the bed. He spread her knees, his fingers going between her thighs to stroke her clit.

Shadow moaned into his mouth as the pads of his fingertips caressed her. His touch was assertive and knowing, moving up and down, then delving into her. Nipping her lips, he slid another finger inside her and licked a path down her neck to her breasts, pausing to nibble at her throbbing pulse. Her nipples were hard nubs, and she let out another moan when his wet, hot mouth covered one. Between the lashing of his tongue and his fingers inside, she exploded in an orgasm. He pushed her thighs farther apart, moved between them, and loomed above her. The blunt head of his cock pushed inside her.

His mouth descended, capturing hers in another hungry kiss. His hips moved, the friction tightening her inner muscles around him. She clung to him, arms going up to his shoulders, her fingers tracing down the muscles of his back. He pounded into her faster. Needy moans escaped her as she met his thrusts. Hands and lips moved everywhere, kissing and touching every bit of skin.

Legs wrapped around him, she dug her heels into his back, urging him to thrust faster and harder. Their lips met again, her mouth opened to him as he devoured her.

Her body went taut. He lifted her hips at just the right angle to send her into orgasm. He shuddered with his pleasure and wrung another orgasm from her before they collapsed, and he disappeared.

SHADOW KNEADED HER fingers in where the swan's skin met his beak, massaging the itchy place for the bird. He sighed, the air expelled from his lungs in a bird-purr. One wing half extended and shook in a ticklish flutter as his body relaxed into her touch. Upright he stood ten feet tall, and his back was broad enough to carry a person, but now he curled around her in a puddle of feathered bliss.

Smiling, she envied the swan's utter pleasure in the simple act — something he would be happy to let her do for him day after day for the rest of his immortal life. She'd performed this service for him countless times and used to take joy in his contentment.

Unfortunately, after her return from her latest kidnapping a week ago, she'd felt different. Whatever spell their mother used to tame them didn't seem to affect her anymore. She still enjoyed caring for the soul birds, but time no longer flew. It dragged each day through an abyss of sameness. She felt like she was getting older and a little part of her died, even as she lived the same day over and over again.

She had to get out of here.

But how? Her mother could track any of her daughters and bring them back. Kidnapped or escaped, they were always returned to the safety of Pohjola. If Mother found out that the taming spell wasn't working anymore, she'd adjust it, and Shadow would fall back into mindless tranquility.

Shadow didn't want to return to that state, afraid she'd remember being awakened, but not be able to wake again. She needed to convince her mother to let her go.

Using her sisters as a distraction, she'd diverted her mother's attention from herself and practiced with shadows. She smiled as Dream and Rainbow joined in caring for the swans, dressed in boots, trousers, and tunics. Their mother would never have the seamstress make such boyish clothing, so Dream had dreamed it up, and Rainbow had given it color. Shadow wasn't the only one learning to use her magic in new ways.

Dream wore shades of yellow, while Rainbow was true to her name — one boot green, the other blue. Red pants and an orange tunic tied with a purple sash. Rainbow had even dared to put a stripe of indigo in her hair! She changed the hue with her mood.

Shadow bit her lip. All those colors would drive their mother mad. She finished her attentions to the swan she was taking care of. The large bird curled his long neck and tucked his beak beneath his wing for a nap.

If Shadow hurried, she could get some practice in while their mother dealt with the man Shadow had encouraged Memory to complain about.

Hurrying to her bedroom, she left the magic ice chandelier off and lit candles instead, creating a legion of shadows in all shapes and sizes. Other than her bed, her room contained a wardrobe and a desk. She'd borrowed knickknacks from her sisters — vases, statues, anything that would throw different shaped shadows onto the walls, and arrayed them on all of the surfaces.

She'd grown faster with her weapons, and no longer needed fury to wield them. Her shadow magic came to her fingertips with a thought. She formed swords, daggers, whips, and shields. The more she used her magic, the more it called to her. What else could she do? As if her magic wanted to show her, one shadow, darker than the rest, drew others to it and formed a rectangular shape. Like a door.

A door. Did her magic work like that? The shadows always felt connected to one another, and she'd reached through one to manipulate another when she fought the Amazon. Could that connection allow her to travel to another place if she stepped in? How far would the shadows take her?

Extending one hand, Shadow pressed her palm against the darkness. New shadows called to her. Whole other parts of the palace opened up to her. In the next room her magic had texture — smooth scales, soft fur, and ruffled feathers. Nature's room. Heat and lightning carried on winds that rumbled like thunder. That had to be Weather. Other shadows slipped through her fingers in less tangible wisps. Dream. Wet shadows ebbed and surged. Tides. Deep shadows were Memory. Clouds of shadow in different shades of dark. Rainbow. Some smelled like flowers and felt like grass to her touch. Spring.

Shadows of the darkest black with so much depth they threatened to drown her, she pulled away from. Without a doubt, those belonged to Mother.

In her excitement, Shadow pressed harder with her magic. Her palm rested against the icy wall behind the shadow. She focused, striving to reach farther away than the rooms immediately next to her.

Her magic responded and grew, doubling and redoubling, not only in size but in power. The wall behind her shadow disappeared, and she staggered forward. Blinking, she stared. The wall hadn't vanished, but her hand and arm had — straight into the shadow.

A flood of new sensations rushed to her. Shadows, ethereal but loyal things, ignored and taken for granted, all tried to outdo one another as they basked in her attention. They showed her what they saw and felt every day, whispering secrets and inviting her to join them.

Shadow stepped forward and held up her other arm. Both limbs entered the darkness up to her shoulders. Another step and her leg vanished. One more step and she entered a new world made of ever-changing shadows.

The dark shapes overlapped and writhed. Light flickered through randomly shaped portals. A small candle here. Another rectangular door outlined by light on the opposite side. Murmurs of conversation carried indistinct words. The sitting room she shared with her sisters?

Yes. The textures of the shadows told her Winter, Healing, Weaver, Night, and Day were there. She held back the shout of joy. What if they could hear her when she used her magic like this?

Shadow sent tendrils out to explore this new world. To the right, where the soul birds wandered outside in their grassy meadow, bird-shaped shadows preened one another, or lay curled in lumps with their heads tucked under their wings. She formed a hand at the end of one tendril and stroked a soul bird's head. The sensation of silky feathers moving under her palm sent a thrill through her, and the swan rumbled his bird-purr.

At an even greater distance, the shadows smelled of evergreen and cool, soft, springy spikes brushed her fingers. The forest! She could reach so far!

Turning the other way, Shadow sent coils into the palace. They connected with other shadows and still more... until they arrived at a protected place in the deepest part of her home. Her mother's vault.

No one knew what the Goddess of Witchcraft and Death kept in there. Rumors abounded. Heaps of treasure. The preserved bodies of the men who tried to kidnap her daughters.

Anything was possible.

Behind her, and far away, a fist banged on a door. Shadow whirled. The quick movement disoriented her, and she stumbled out of the shadow she'd entered. The way all the shadows moved over one another changed all the entrances and exits.

"Shadow," Memory hissed. "Are you in there?"

It would be easy to get lost in this shadow world if she went to unfamiliar places, but Memory was at Shadow's bedroom door. She searched for the deep shadows that felt like her sister and touched the layers of shadow between them, sifting until she found the one leading back.

"Yes. Just a second." Would Memory hear that?

"Hurry up!"

It worked! Shadow emerged into her bedroom and waved a hand at the crystal chandelier, activating the bright light in the room before she opened the door.

Memory looked furtively over her shoulder down the hallway and slinked into the room. "I did it. I told Mother about the old man."

"Good. Did she tell him he had to leave?"

"No. I listened outside the door." Memory shook her head. "He offered her something called a Sampo and said his brother would come here to make it. But she had him thrown in the dungeon until she gets her prize."

That was not part of the plan. She thought when Mother caught Väinämöinen, she would assign him a quest. He would refuse to do it, because he was arrogant, and try to kidnap one of them. He had a calculating, condescending attitude, but she'd made a point of flattering him so he knew which sister she was. She hadn't expected her mother to jail him. But while it put a crimp in her plan, it was only a delay. All she had to do was make sure he took the right sister when he was freed.

In the meantime, she could practice her magic. Maybe it was time to find out what Mother kept in her vault.

CHAPTER FOUR

LOUHI

VÄINÄMÖINEN HAD OVERESTIMATED his brother's abilities. After the week it took him to arrive in the first place, with an uninvited apprentice no less, Ilmarinen took three more days to set up his forge, even with his helper, Kullervo.

To Louhi's surprise, she quite liked the ferocious, black-eyed, wild boy with his shock of unruly black hair. He looked like he'd never used a brush or a comb in all ten years of his life. The fearless little scamp bared his teeth at her and spoke without stammering, or an excessive use of pronouns. He was a refreshing change from the heroes, princes, and villains who regularly showed up to kidnap a Maiden of Pohjola. She might have to keep him after she murdered Ilmarinen and his brother.

Which seemed more likely every day.

The endless ringing of hammer on anvil had seemed to indicate an appropriate level of enthusiasm by Ilmarinen to complete his task. But his general incompetence, and inappropriate infatuation with Rainbow, which for some reason she returned, addled his brain. *I suppose if you like the hulking, bearded type, he's not so bad.* Her winds had reported him gentle and conscientious when he interacted with Rainbow.

Good thing for him, because if he lifted a single finger or said a hurtful word, Louhi would use his blacksmith's hammer for things it had never been used for before.

But their infatuation had resulted in mistake after mistake.

A deadly bow had flown into the throne room and tried to kill her, the Mistress of Pohjola, of all people.

A warship rampaged in the harbor.

A savage cow ran amok in the forest.

And, a murderous plow tore up the swan's meadow and terrified the birds.

Skillful blacksmith. Ha!

Chaos had destroyed the peace of her orderly, pristine realm. Her increasingly rebellious daughters only added to the ruckus, their giggling and dramatics encouraging the clumsy behavior of the smith — to the point Louhi questioned whether it was deliberate at this point.

It was enough to drive a Goddess of Witchcraft and Death to drink her mother's strongest Beer of Oblivion. Time to bring down a hammer of her own. Louhi took her hag form and stormed into the forge. "Ilmarinen!" she thundered. "List your pronouns."

The smith, eyes focused out the window on Rainbow again, hadn't noticed Louhi's approach, even in her hag form. He jumped, his heavy hammer skidding off the hot metal he was pointlessly banging on. Hot sparks flew up and landed in his beard and curly hair the color of the mud she'd reduce him to if he didn't complete his work soon. He frantically patted out the embers, but in his flailing, dropped a bottle of something into the fire. Blue, purple, red, orange, yellow, and green flames leapt up.

A gift from Rainbow in thanks for one of the many presents he'd bestowed on her, no doubt.

Startling the oaf may have been a miscalculation. *I hope that doesn't result in yet another mistake.* Louhi stalked forward. *A rainbow-colored mistake.* A headache bloomed behind her right eye.

"I... you —"

"Excellent. Those are quite enough pronouns. You have been here nearly two weeks and there is no sign of my Sampo."

"I —"

"Perhaps if you kept your eyes on your work rather than my daughter, you could make some worthwhile progress."

Ilmarinen swallowed, eyes darting toward the window.

"She is why you are here, is she not? Your brother promised her to you as a reward, didn't he? Coveting your prize before you've finished your work?"

Outraged gasps came from Rainbow and Shadow, where they had moved to hide below the window Ilmarinen kept glancing out.

The smith straightened. "I... She... no!"

"Your brother did not promise you my daughter as a reward?"

"Well —"

"Did he or did he not?" Louhi bellowed.

He hung his head. "He did."

She almost believed he actually was sorry.

Rainbow stood from her hiding place and burst into tears. Shadow also stood, sliding an arm around her sister's shoulders, murmuring comforting words. Rainbow lifted her head high, stomped into the forge, and glared at Ilmarinen. "I never want to see you again! You're just like all the others!"

She jerked at a chain around her neck and threw a pendant in the smith's face, then drew back her blue-booted foot to kick him in the shin. Her green boot stomped on his toes.

Perhaps the words Shadow whispered hadn't been words of comfort after all.

As much as Louhi abhorred the sound of booted feet in her palace, she had to admit the new footwear of her daughters made for more effective stomping and kicking than delicate, quiet slippers.

Shadow aimed a withering glower at the smith and led Rainbow away. Ilmarinen's shoulders sagged, and a stricken expression crossed his face.

"Do you think you can concentrate on your work now?" Louhi asked.

"That was cruel."

"More cruel than treating her as a possession and letting her think she has no more value than as payment for your services rendered?"

"She didn't think that until you threw it in her face just now." He didn't look at her as he spoke, but there was some heat in his words.

Louhi arched an eyebrow. Perhaps the smith had some spine, after all. He must have learned some things from his apprentice.

"So you would just have let her believe she meant something to you? Would you have ever told her the truth?"

Ilmarinen raised his eyes and met her gaze unflinchingly. "I care for her. That is the truth. And I thought she cared for me, until a moment ago. I came to save my brother, not to claim a woman who doesn't want me. That's never worked out for Väinämöinen. I hoped I could impress her. That she might welcome my affection."

"So you had no intention of leaving Pohjola with any of my daughters?"

"No. Not unless she wants to come with me." Ilmarinen lifted his hammer. "I'll finish your Sampo, take my brother, and leave this place."

Not so much spine then. He wouldn't fight for Rainbow. With a sigh, Louhi turned to leave.

"The work would go faster if my apprentice was available to do his job."

Like she would allow that spirited boy back into the hands of men such as Ilmarinen and his brother. "He is otherwise engaged. Finish without him. Quickly."

The renewed metallic banging of the hammer had an extra volume to it, jarring her nerves with every impact. To deaden the sound, and keep her daughters away, Louhi summoned the four winds to fan the flames and surround the forge.

Three days later, the smith emerged, Sampo in hand. The little mill produced grain, salt, and gold on command, as agreed. Louhi locked it in her vault, released Väinämöinen from his cell, and lounged on her throne in anticipation of quiet and order restored.

"We're here to claim two of your daughters." Väinämöinen made the pronouncement, swaggering into her throne room as if he expected her to obey him. Ilmarinen hung back, shaking his head.

Louhi leaned back on her throne. "I think not. I offered the choice of one of my daughters to you. You offered one of my daughters to your brother."

Väinämöinen stroked his beard. "I am still owed my choice. You kept me in the dungeon for weeks! You cannot think I endured that treatment and will not demand recompense."

So tedious. "Fine. As per our deal, you may choose one of my daughters." She closed her eyes, fighting the beginning of a headache. "So name your choice."

Väinämöinen inhaled, no doubt to proclaim his decree to the world. But no words were forthcoming. His teeth clacked together when he closed his mouth.

"You didn't even ask their names, did you?" Louhi opened her eyes and gave him a big gap-toothed grin. "My daughters will remain here."

"Sky! I'll take the one named Sky. She wears silver and gold, and walks in purple clouds."

Louhi tsked. "She is the very same one you offered to your brother, isn't she? Her name isn't Sky, but we have some lovely parting gifts. Like your lives." She waved a hand, dismissing the men from her presence. The headache was blooming.

The old man took two steps forward, pointed a gnarled finger at her and lowered his voice. "But you know which one I chose."

"That is true. Although, even if you knew her name, I didn't say you could take her with you, only that you could choose. Which you have done. I'd never force any of my daughters to marry someone she didn't want to be with."

"So we are to have none of them?" Väinämöinen's voice dropped to a growl.

Louhi lifted one shoulder in a shrug. "Even if I was going to let you take one, you bartered the daughter you could have had to your brother to create the Sampo, so you are no longer entitled to one. Your brother accepted her refusal to leave with him, so he has no claim on any of them, either. I will still honor the part of our bargain where I keep the Sampo, and you leave Pohjola alive. Amaze me with your pronouns one last time and get out."

"You... you..." He curled his hands into fists. "You deceitful witch!"

Louhi waggled her fingers.

He turned and stormed out. For a moment Ilmarinen paused, but he followed his brother without a word.

Crossing to a window overlooking the front of her castle, she waited. Which of her daughters would it be this time? Memory? For all her remembering everything that ever happened in Pohjola, she forgot her common sense at the chance to be kidnapped. Dream? She was always relying on a handsome man to make her dreams come true rather than working herself. Perhaps Rainbow. That girl always had her head in the clouds, but she hadn't forgiven the smith for breaking her heart.

Laughter and cries of outrage filled the air.

"Stop it!"

"You're handsome. Do you have a big... horse?"

"Hey! Get your hands off me!"

"It's not her turn!"

"Put me down!"

The fun was about to begin. Maybe that would get rid of this blasted headache.

CHAPTER FIVE

SHADOW

THEIR SITTING ROOM was a disaster. Furniture overturned. Glasses and dishes smashed on the floor. Torn gowns. Sisters running in all directions. Shadow regretted introducing boots to her sisters when her shin took a hard kick from Memory. Soul birds crowded at the window, watching the anarchy with hissing sounds and feathers on their heads standing upright.

Twelve women vying for their turn to be kidnapped put up a lot more fight than one Amazon. Shadow looped dark tendrils of her magic around a shrieking Spring and swept her into a corner to hide her from view with seven of their other sisters. Shadow ducked as a vase flew at her head, shattering on the wall when it missed her.

It took all her concentration to keep the sisters she'd already caught from breaking free while she tried to corral the last ones. "Trust me! This will work out for all of us. You'll see."

If her plan worked. If it didn't, her life in Pohjola would become a lot less boring, but a lot more miserable. Memory was already angry with her. All her sisters were, but Memory's ire was something neither party would ever forget.

"You think he's a creepy old man!" Memory aimed another kick at Shadow. "Why do you want to go, anyway?"

"I have a plan, Memory. You can have my next turn."

"Your next turn isn't for ages!"

A clock ticked in Shadow's mind. The countdown to her bid for independence. It had taken more time than she'd thought to break into her mother's vault and steal the Sampo. She'd honed her skill with her shadows as weapons. Using them as keys to pick magical locks had been trickier.

Her mother would come for her at some point. The Goddess of Witchcraft and Death always brought her daughters home. But Shadow needed to show off her new abilities for fighting and defending herself *now*. Prove she didn't need to be taken care of. All of her progress and planning would be ruined if she failed now and her mother just showed up for the rescue later.

Stealing Louhi's possessions was a sure way to get her immediate attention.

Ilmarinen and his brother were in Mother's throne room. They'd be on their way here soon to take what they thought was theirs, and she still had four sisters to get safely out of the way.

Väinämöinen and Ilmarinen burst into their sitting room and paused, taking in the pandemonium. Weaver dashed toward Ilmarinen. "You're handsome. Do you have a big... horse?"

Shadow rolled her eyes and created two dark hands. They closed around Weaver and scooped her up.

"Hey!" Weaver struggled against their grip. "Get your hands off me!"

Dream pressed against the wall, trying to sidle past unnoticed. A whip of shadow snapped around Dream's waist and pulled her into the air. It receded into the wall, dragging her with it. "Put me down!"

Ilmarinen eyed Rainbow. A shadow from the wall crept along the floor to pool in a circle around her feet and flow up her legs.

"Stop it!" Rainbow screeched, waving an arm for Ilmarinen. He reached for her outstretched hand.

Nope. That was not happening. Thinking he could take her sister in trade for an object, no matter how rare, was worse than kidnapping! But Shadow couldn't let any of her sisters be taken. Mother wouldn't consider that a win. All the sisters had to be safe.

Her mother's vault. They'd be safe there.

Reaching through the shadows holding her sisters prisoner, to one she remembered in the vault, Shadow staggered as her magic siphoned out of her, forging a connection between the two places. With a jolt, the pull on her power released, leaving an umbral tunnel. Rainbow disappeared into the floor with a scream. Ilmarinen's hands closed over air.

Memory gaped, then made a run for Ilmarinen. Shadow intercepted her and elbowed her aside. Reeling from the blow, Memory stepped in a shadow, trying to regain her balance. "It's not her turn!"

Shadow summoned shadows until they crowded the room, shrouding the rest of her sisters. Then, she shoved, and the rest of them vanished as the surrounding darkness contracted with a pop. Gasping, she teetered and fell to her hands and knees. Her sisters were all safe, but she had used almost all her magic.

A hand closed over her arm, wrenching her up to kneeling. "Oh, no you don't. You're coming with us." Väinämöinen manhandled her until he could toss her over his shoulder, letting out a yelp as the Sampo jabbed him. Dropping her to the floor, he searched her until he found the little windmill, tossed it to his brother, and levered Shadow back over his shoulder. "Let's go."

She would not miss being hauled around like this. Garnering her strength, she bided her time until she had to fight again.

CHAPTER SIX

LOUHI

VÄINÄMÖINEN BURST OUT of the castle gate, a willowy blonde draped over his shoulder.

Louhi laughed. He'd have his hands full with Shadow. Of all her daughters, Shadow was the least empty-headed when it came to muscle-bound oafs, nice singing voices or not. Especially since she'd returned from her last outing.

She stopped laughing when Ilmarinen followed his brother. He didn't carry one of her daughters, though. He carried her Sampo. It was all part of the fun and games for men to sneak into Pohjola and try for her daughters. It was the reason she left the borders so open. Stealing her possessions, though — that changed everything.

Storming through the castle, Louhi let her magic build.

Shadow was the most aware, but she'd never become what Louhi suspected she could be if she remained here. Living in Pohjola kept her daughters innocent and child-like. The easier it was for them to entertain themselves, the fewer complaints Louhi had to deal with. Like the inevitable griping she'd have from all her other daughters if she gave

Shadow the chance she needed. Was her daughter ready to face the human world again?

That world had nearly destroyed Shadow once, and Louhi had let a man with twin scimitars exact vengeance for her daughter. If humans tried to hurt her daughter again, Louhi would take gryphon form and show them exactly what the Goddess of Witchcraft and Death could do.

Seeing Shadow so nearly broken when she'd returned from that long ago kidnapping may have caused Louhi to become a little overprotective, but perhaps Shadow had outgrown the need for such drastic measures.

Maybe it was time to stop protecting her.

"You killed my son!" A wailing woman clutched at Louhi's arm as she threw open balcony doors.

Louhi tried to pull free, but the woman had an impressive grip. "I haven't killed anyone." Well, that wasn't true. She had, but not lately. She thought for a second and added, "Recently."

"Lemminki is dead!"

"Lemming?" All he had to do was bring her a feather! Although, it had been a few weeks since she'd told him to do that. "I didn't kill him."

"He drowned in the river in Tuonela!"

The headache forming behind Louhi's eyes and in her temples, exploded. How had that gone so wrong? Were there no competent men anymore? She didn't have time for this. Brushing by the woman, Louhi leapt onto the balcony railing.

"This is your fault! I want my son back!"

The only things worse than incompetent heroes were their meddling mothers. "I need to attend to something right now. I'll be right back."

"My son!"

"If he's dead now, he'll still be dead when I return, won't he?" Louhi shifted to her enormous gryphon form and soared into the air. Her powerful wings beat and her hair streamed behind her as she flew after the men dashing for the wharf.

Maybe I should have left that warship alone.

Preparing to dive on her targets, cries of pain — male cries of pain, and cursing made her pull up and hover instead. Louhi conjured an illusion of cloud around herself and watched, curious to see what Shadow was doing. Perhaps she was wearing a pair of those awful boots.

In front of the dock, Väinämöinen and Ilmarinen each hopped on one foot, hands clutched around their opposite knee.

Shadow, magnificent in her fury, stood in front of the injured men. "I told you I don't want to go with you!"

"What you want doesn't matter!" Väinämöinen snarled. "I want a wife, and Ilmarinen is owed for forging the Sampo. You're coming with us."

"I'm not! And, by the way, your voice sounds like a croaky frog with a sore throat!" Magic roiled around Shadow and she pointed at the ground, feeding power into dark shapes.

When had her innocent darling learned to do that? The shadows of Väinämöinen and Ilmarinen drew back and snapped forward, each man's shadow striking the other man's knee.

Louhi gnawed on a talon. Living in Pohjola for so long hadn't done Shadow's ability to hurl insults much good, or taught her how to fight to win, either.

The men bellowed more cries of pain that were cut off as their shadows grabbed one another's throats, throttling each other.

Ah, that was more like it. Louhi smirked. Yes, maybe it was time to find a way to let Shadow grow beyond what she could become here.

Väinämöinen reached for Shadow, but Ilmarinen's shadow let go of Väinämöinen's throat and punched his face. He staggered back, his shadow releasing Ilmarinen.

"Let's get out of here! These women are all crazy!" Ilmarinen limped past his brother, giving Shadow a wide berth. "We have the Sampo. If the witch wants it back, she can bargain for it with us in Kalevala where we're not at her mercy."

"Ha! Mother will come for you long before you make it to Kalevala." Shadow threw out her hands. Ropes of her magic flowed from her fingers, one aimed at each man, coiling around their ankles and cinching, knocking them to the ground.

Shadow turned and stormed up the path to the castle. She looked exhausted, but that was to be expected when using magic in new ways. Louhi laughed. Shadow had been honing her magic, and learning new tricks, right under her nose. The rebellion had been an excellent distraction.

Feet bound, Väinämöinen dragged himself aboard their wooden boat. Ilmarinen slithered on the pier and untied the mooring lines, then hauled himself aboard.

Väinämöinen plucked a few notes on his kantele, and wind filled their sails. Their shadow bonds vanished as they pulled away from the dock and the men clambered to their feet.

Louhi struck like lightning from the sky. She knocked Ilmarinen to the deck and hoped he'd stay down. This wasn't his fault. His brother had begged him to help, and he respected Rainbow's decision, although not happily. And no one had dared steal from her before. He deserved a little respect for gumption, and might have made a suitable match if circumstances had been different.

Väinämöinen deserved no such consideration. The nerve of the man, offering her daughters as payment, treating them like the trinkets he made his brother create for him.

Louhi raked his chest with her clawed feet. He screamed and fell back. She landed on the side of the boat, tipping it low toward the waterline. The sea rushed in, almost swamping the craft.

"Stop!" Ilmarinen held the Sampo over the side. "Let us leave in peace or I'll drop the Sampo!"

"I only agreed to alive. I didn't specify in peace!" Louhi lunged at Ilmarinen, gathering his tunic in her talons. She lifted him, holding him in the air. His feet dangled above the water. "The Sampo belongs to me.

If I can't have it, let it rest at the bottom of the ocean. You won't use it to control me."

Panicked, his fingers spasmed open, and the Sampo vanished beneath the waves. She tossed him after it and landed hard on the bottom of the boat. She dragged her talons through the wood, leaving fissures the water rushed to fill.

"Ilmarinen!" Väinämöinen yelled, reaching out an arm.

Louhi laughed and flapped her wings. She took to the air, making the boat rock again, and flew back toward her castle.

WHERE WERE ALL HER daughters? Louhi had expected to find them with their noses pressed to a window to watch the display, or, more likely, scattering from their spying in an effort to pretend innocence, but they were all conspicuously absent. She had to find Shadow. Her daughter seemed unharmed, but Louhi had let Shadow down once before.

Louhi cornered Shadow in her bedroom. "You cost me the Sampo!"

"You cost me five thousand years of my life!"

Shadow looked as shocked at the words as Louhi felt, but her newly bold daughter went on. "I got away before you arrived, Mother." She crossed her arms. "I was fine."

Louhi snorted. "You girls are always swanning off to fall in love with fools, and getting kidnapped. I can't get anything done with all the rescuing and help you require."

"What if I could prove I can live by myself without being kidnapped? If I can live in the human world without help or needing to be rescued for a hundred years, you'll allow me to come and go from Pohjola without interference."

Louhi tapped a finger on her chin as she mulled the offer over. It would be nice to get these girls out from underfoot. But a hundred years wasn't long enough for her girls to learn to be responsible for themselves after five thousand years of being coddled.

"A thousand years," she countered. "And you can't accept help."

Shadow's jaw dropped. "A *thousand!*"

"No. A thousand and one years. I heard something about a thousand and one years before. Or maybe it was nights. Whatever. I like that number."

"Mother!"

"If you don't think you can do it, we'll forget this conversation ever happened." Louhi held her breath, willing her most headstrong daughter to believe in herself.

After a long moment, Shadow lifted her chin. "No. I accept your terms. I will live in the human world for a thousand and one years, without accepting help or needing to be rescued. But when I succeed, I'm free to come and go from Pohjola without interference of any kind, and you have to let my sisters have a chance to be free."

Louhi wanted to cheer, but only gave a nod to Shadow. She conjured a satchel and held it out to her daughter. "Agreed. Pack what you need. Until our deal is over, broken or completed, you cannot come back here."

Shadow collected clothing and jewelry, which she placed in the satchel. "Can I say goodbye to my sisters? They... they won't understand and will be angry with me."

And have to deal with all the tears and moping for days? Louhi did not want to deal with the fallout from the drama long goodbyes would entail. "No. Better you make a clean break of it and go before they figure out what's happened. But I'll allow communication between you in the human world and your sisters here."

Finished packing, Shadow nodded, glanced around her room, and stood rooted to the spot.

"Well? What are you waiting for?" *Be brave, Shadow. You can do this. I won't let what happened to you before happen ever again.*

In an action clearly learned in the human world, Shadow rolled her eyes. "The portal to the human world?"

"So willing to accept help already? I don't see this bargain lasting long. I'll make sure your place at the dinner table is ready for your return."

Shadow's eyes widened. "No! I don't need your portal. I'll go by myself." Glaring, she stepped into the nearest shadow and folded it over herself.

Louhi smiled and sent a wisp of wind with Shadow to watch over her as she disappeared. Their bargain said Shadow couldn't accept help, but that didn't mean Louhi couldn't provide it if Shadow remained none the wiser.

Holding out one hand as she paced the corridor to her throne room, the Goddess of Witchcraft and Death whispered an incantation. The Sampo appeared in her hand. Nothing in Pohjola was beyond her reach, even things at the bottom of the sea.

"Mother!" Memory's angry voice carried down the hallway.

"What is it, Memory?"

"Shadow took my turn! She got to go last time, and she elbowed me out of the way. Then her shadows went crazy, and she said she had a plan and to trust her, but —"

"What do you mean, her shadows went crazy? Did she hurt you?"

"No, but she made Rainbow disappear into the floor, pinned us to walls and made her shadows swallow us, so we went from our sitting room to your vault!" Memory stamped her foot. "And she took my turn!"

So, Shadow was more crafty than Louhi had given her credit for. Ilmarinen didn't deserve any respect for stealing from the vault after all. Shadow did. And there were depths to her new magic and the way she wielded it Louhi hadn't expected.

"Don't worry, Memory. I've made sure Shadow won't be stealing your turn anymore."

Memory's face eased from angry lines to the smooth, timeless beauty each of her daughters had. An eerie, ethereal beauty that meant they'd never had to worry about a thing. How would Shadow's face be different next time Louhi saw it? Careworn and drawn? Not so beautiful anymore?

No, there was a look that came with being independent and living free. Beautiful as they were, and as easy as she made their lives, none of her daughters would ever have that look in Pohjola. But she hoped to see it on Shadow's face when she looked in on her next — she wanted to see her daughter happy.

"Thank you, Mother."

Louhi accepted the thanks and the kiss on her cheek before Memory scampered from the room.

She relaxed into her throne as her headache eased. One daughter down. She mulled over ideas for how she could teach the rest of them that they only needed themselves. Where had Shadow learned it? Louhi would have to figure out who had kidnapped Shadow last and find out more about him. Maybe she could screen potential kidnappers and make things easier for ones like him.

"My son is still dead!" A woman's shrill voice ripped through her reverie. "What do you intend to do about that?"

Louhi sighed, her headache rushing back.

At least the mothers of hapless heroes could speak in more than pronouns.

CHAPTER SEVEN

SHADOW

SHADOW HAD THE PRIZE she wanted, but what to do with it? Had she only wanted the challenge of winning her freedom as a way to stave off boredom, and now she would be bored again? No, she could set herself an unlimited number of challenges — she never had to be bored.

Freedom with no limits was daunting.

And tiring. Instead of one portal to the human world, it had taken over twenty shadow steps, each a little farther than the last. As she mastered this part of her magic, sensing shadows beyond her immediate area and pulling herself in the direction of her ultimate destination, her strength drained faster than she expected.

She needed a place to rest. Somewhere hidden and empty, so no one knew she was there. Shadow altered her course slightly, reaching for lonely shadows — the ones that formed and traveled over the same ground day after day without interruption. Better not to see anyone else right now.

Her magic slipped from her grasp and dropped her out of the Shadow world. She staggered, hit a wall and slid to the cold, hard floor of wherever her shadows had dropped her.

Shadow blinked. Some sort of dungeon. Chains ending in manacles hung from the walls and snaked along the floor. She needed to rest, but terror set her heart pounding and stopped her breathing. A sensation of cold metal locked around her ankle and pulled her arms behind her back.

A window was barred. The wooden door hung open. There was a way out. Her arms weren't trapped. She wasn't shackled.

She'd never been imprisoned in a place like this. Surely, if something like that happened to her, she'd remember, wouldn't she?

A man with a dark bushy beard streaked with white raised his hand to strike her.

Men tore at her clothing, laughing and jeering.

Her mother would never have allowed that sort of treatment. So why was she remembering those things?

Two curved swords rose and fell. A hooded man held the blades as he whirled and slashed at attackers. When his black eyes landed on her, a shiver of anticipation ran through her.

Through the bars of her cell, her shadow lover skimmed his hand over her belly to her hip, then up her bare thigh, sending hot jolts through her. Arms bound behind her, all she could do was lift her hips in invitation.

Her mouth opened in surprise, and his tongue slid in to catch her gasp when a thick finger thrust into her center. He rubbed his thumb against her clit and spread that wetness before dipping a second finger into her. Her inner muscles gripped his fingers as he moved them within her.

He moved his fingers in a different way, and his palm rubbed against her. She ground against his hand as he pushed her closer and closer to the edge.

Coiling tension built within her. She moaned into his mouth, receiving one of his low growls in return. His fingers moved faster inside her. He curled them and increased the pressure of his thumb circling on her clit. She lifted onto her toes when her orgasm took her.

Spots danced in her vision. They didn't go away when she closed her eyes. All at once, her lungs worked, and she sucked in a breath. Forget trying to rest here. The need to get where she was going urged her on.

And who was that man? She would never have forgotten meeting someone like him, would she? He'd never come to Pohjola. All her sisters would have talked about someone like him. Why did he make her feel so... safe and wanted?

Why did she want him? She'd never felt that way about any of her kidnappers. A sense of completeness and devotion. Tears rose in her eyes and she sniffled.

Horrified, she swiped the tears away. She'd only left Pohjola ten minutes ago, and already she was crying like the helpless girl she didn't want to be anymore.

She had to learn to do things for herself, no matter how those black eyes drew her in. He was imaginary. He had to be. Just wishful thinking because she was alone for the first time. No home to go back to. No sisters around. No mother to take care of her.

This dungeon was depressing her, that was all. It was a disheartening sort of place.

Magic flagging, she pushed back into the shadow world, holding the passage together with sheer will as she pulled herself toward the distant familiar shadows.

She was almost there.

And she'd done it without help.

Almost.

Finally, within her reach — damp, gritty, and shifting shadows, salt-tinged from the breeze, and warmed from the sun.

Shadow summoned the last of her energy, hauling her body through the shadow tunnel. She'd made it! Letting go of her shadows to exit into the human world, she fell rather than stepped and swallowed sea water as she landed in a frigid ocean with a splash.

Watch that last step.

Sputtering, Shadow kicked to the surface, her satchel floating next to her. The rocky island and castle she was aiming for loomed in front of her, and she swam the short distance to shore. Crawling onto the soft, shifting sandy beach, she turned onto her back and looked at the blue sky.

The sun seemed brighter. The air smelled fresher. Even the sand rubbing her in places where sand shouldn't be rubbing anybody didn't feel as abrasive as it should.

She was free. Closing her eyes, she reveled in the moment.

A shadow not hers blocked the sun. Shadow opened her eyes.

The Amazon stood over her "Och. Bampot radges just wash up all over the place." She extended a hand.

Their familiar positioning made Shadow smile. How many times had they been exactly like this when she was learning to fight?

Shadow reached up, then jerked her fingers back to the sand. Her blood ran cold. Would even such an insignificant gesture as letting the Amazon pull her to her feet be considered accepting help? The carelessly worded bargain dominated her thoughts. No wonder her mother had been so accommodating when she agreed to their deal.

Belatedly, she reproached herself. The Amazon had taught her better. Shadow should have been more specific. Made their bargain about her *asking* for help, not accepting help. Now if anyone did anything for her, her mother could consider their deal broken and Shadow would end up right back in Pohjola.

Well, poorly worded bargain or not, she wouldn't give her mother the excuse to cage her again.

Hands on her hips now, the Amazon frowned. "Lass, do ye need help up?"

"No." Shadow laughed. "I can do it myself." As she pushed herself to her feet, determination gave her resolve. She would control shadows, but she would *be* Shadow no longer. She would be... victorious.

She made another decision without help.

And named herself Viktoria.

THE END

THANK YOU

Thank you for sticking with the story to the end! If you enjoyed it, please consider leaving a review. A couple of words, or even just a rating from you can help others find my work, which will encourage me to write more stories!

ABOUT THE AUTHOR

I love to travel, read, and think of ways to complicate my characters' lives. I have two borrowed cats who take shameless advantage of my good nature. Hopefully you find my characters a lot more entertaining than I am. :)

If you enjoyed this story, you may be interested to know that I write in several series. While each novel is written for one relationship, features unique mythologies, and can be read as standalone, a little more of that world is revealed and the overall arc of the series grows throughout.

The best way to find out what's going on with the series, and me, is to visit my website at https://www.ysobellablack.com. There, you can check out the wikis and timelines for each series. Or, sign up for the newsletter.

https://ysobellablack.com/newsletter/

I send out things like surveys, freebies, contests, and random news about things going on with me that may or may not be interesting.

I love hearing from my readers. Feel free to send me an email at ysobella@ysobellablack.com.

Or find me here:

Twitter[1]

Pinterest[2]

Goodreads[3]

Instagram[4]

---

1. https://twitter.com/ysobellablack

2. https://pinterest.com/ysobellablack/

3. https://www.goodreads.com/ysobellablack

4. https://www.instagram.com/ysobellablackauthor/

<u>TikTok</u>[5]
<u>Bookbub</u>[6]

---

5. http://www.tiktok.com/ysobellablack

6. http://www.bookbub.com/ysobellablack

Written as Ysobel Black
(Nice/Sweet Versions)

Bakery Street Cozy Mysteries
Paranormal Cozy Mysteries
The Lyrical Lycanthrope

Fairy Tales With a Twist
Retellings of fairy tales, myths, and stories you only thought you knew.
The Crimson Hood & the Alpha of Wolves
The Ice Maiden & the Princes of Diamonds

Holiday Hullabaloo
Love in Ashana can be tricky, but twelve days of chaos result in
paranormal happily-ever-afters.
A Penghou in a Pine Tree
Two Tatzelwurms
Three French Bêtes
Four Ceffyl Dŵr
Five Golden Wings
Six Grootslangs Playing

Seven Spawns a-Swimming
Eight Maenads Mixing
Nine Lazy Dragons
Ten Swords a-Sneaking
Eleven Pixie Potions
Twelve Lovers Loving

Pohjola Maidens

The Maidens of Pohjola are free, heading for the human world, and looking for love.
Dream's Sleeper: Lemminki

Strygoi Witches & Vampires

Join an Ildum of vampires over 10,000 years of history and mythology as they find their Dragăs — witches who make their hearts beat and restore their souls..
Ember's Light: Stryx
Viktoria's Shadow: Jael
Myth's Legend: Norrix
Bijou's Cure: Zeke
Musette's Fate: Idris

Strygoi Witches & Vampires Companion Stories

Shadowy — Viktoria's prequel (companion novella)
Echo's Answer: Lachlan (companion novel)

COLLECTIONS/BOX SETS

Holiday Hullabaloo
DAYS 1-12

Strygoi Witches & Vampires
COLLECTION ONE: BOOKS 1-4

Written as Ysobella Black (Naughty/ Steamy Versions)

Alix in Wonderland

A reverse harem (MFMMM) retelling of Alice in Wonderland.
Madness of the Hatter

Bakery Street Mysteries

Paranormal Cozy-ish Mysteries
The Lyrical Lycanthrope

Fairy Tales With a Kink

Retellings of fairy tales, myths, and stories you only thought you knew.
The Crimson Hood & the Alpha of Wolves
The Ice Maiden & the Princes of Diamonds

Grove of Bandrui

Immortal Druids search for their Maités.
Druid of Oaks
Druid of Apples

Harom & Aneja

Witches choose three men to form their Haroms as they become Aneja
— Walkers in magic. Reverse Harem (MFMM)
RealmWalker
BeastWalker

Magical Love in London

Regency London with a paranormal twist.
Marriage of Inconvenience

Oubliette

Paranormal short and steamy stories.
Selkie
Merrow

Pohjola Passions

The Maidens of Pohjola are free, on their way to the human world, and
looking for love.
Dream's Sleeper: Lemminki

Raven Chronicles: Phoenix Rising

The battle for the Raven Throne in the Inisfail Fae Court is full of war,
sex, and intrigue that spans generations.

First Generation

Souls Lost & Found

Once in a blue moon, star-crossed lovers get a second chance for their love to shine.
The Egyptian

Utopia Pack

A pack of shifters find their Fateds.
Unyielding

Vampires & Strygoi Witches

Join an Ildum of vampires over 10,000 years of history and mythology as they find their Dragăs — witches who make their hearts beat and restore their souls.
Ember's Light: Stryx
Viktoria's Shadow: Jael
Myth's Legend: Norrix
Bijou's Cure: Zeke
Musette's Fate: Idris

Vampires & Strygoi Witches Companion Stories

Shadowy — Viktoria's Prequel
Echo's Answer: Lachlan

Xov & Xau

In a war where each side is determined to inherit the earth, sparks fly.
And when Xov finds Xau, a different sort of sparks ignite.
Poisoned Heart

Yuletide Chaos

Love in Ashana can be tricky, but twelve days of chaos result in
paranormal happily-ever-afters.
A Penghou in a Pine Tree
Two Tatzelwurms
Three French Bêtes
Four Ceffyl Dŵr
Five Golden Wings
Six Grootslangs Playing
Seven Spawns a-Swimming
Eight Maenads Mixing
Nine Lazy Dragons
Ten Swords a-Sneaking
Eleven Pixie Potions
Twelve Lovers Loving

COLLECTIONS/BOX SETS

Three First in a Series

FATED – Three Firsts

Ember's Light:Stryx
RealmWalker
Poisoned Heart

Five First in a Series

FATED – Five Firsts
Ember's Light:Stryx
The Crimson Hood & the Alpha of Wolves
RealmWalker
Dream's Sleeper: Lemminki
Poisoned Heart

Vampires & Strygoi Witches

COLLECTION ONE: BOOKS 1-4

Yuletide Yearnings

Yuletide Chaos, Days 1-12

PAGE * MERGEFORMAT 1

www.ingramcontent.com/pod-product-compliance
Lightning Source LLC
Chambersburg PA
CBHW061357160726
47995CB00001B/357